For Elizabeth & Jack
Merry Christmas 1999
Flo Dourup

A SPUR for Christmas

Flo Baurys

Illustrated by Gerald L. Holmes

ENCHANTED
❖ ROCK ❖

An imprint of Gulf Publishing Company
Houston, Texas

To my granddaughter Sydnie Colbert.

Because you bear my father's name,

you are my love connection to past

and future generations.

A Spur for Christmas

Enchanted Rock
An imprint of Gulf Publishing Company
Book Division
P.O. Box 2608 □ Houston, Texas 77252-2608

10 9 8 7 6 5 4 3 2 1

Library of Congress Cataloging-in-Publication Data

Baurys, Florence, 1938–
   A spur for Christmas / Flo Baurys ; illustrated by Gerald Holmes.
      p.   cm.
   Summary: Inspired by the Christmas tree in the ranch house, Augie the armadillo and his brothers decide to make their own and proceed to decorate a prickly pear cactus, making a real Texas-style Christmas tree.
   ISBN 0-88415-300-2 (alk. paper)
   [1. Armadillos Fiction. 2. Christmas trees Fiction. 3. Christmas Fiction. 4. Texas Fiction.]
   I. Holmes, Gerald L., ill.   II. Title.
PZ7.B32855Sp   1999
[E]—dc21   99-31005
                                                                 CIP

Printed in Hong Kong.

Printed on acid-free paper (∞).

Black-and-white line drawings electronically colored by Senta Eva Rivera.

Book and cover design by Roxann L. Combs.

"Quick! Come see," said Augie Armadillo.

His three brothers Bud, Clyde, and Duke
followed him to the Jarrett ranch house.

"Up here," Augie said.

The armadillos scampered over the stack of firewood below the parlor window, digging their long, hard nails into the bark to help them climb. The window was covered with frost, and they had to clear a space to see inside.

A tall Christmas tree occupied one end of the room. They stared in amazement at the bright lights, the popcorn strings, the colorful ornaments, and the sparkling star on the tip.

"WOW!" said Clyde.

"Let's make one," Duke said.

"First we need to find a tree."
Augie, the firstborn, always took charge.

The armadillos set out across the west forty,
zigzagging to dodge the tumbleweed that was
blowing about.

Bud was the first to spot a prickly pear cactus
with lots of growth on it. "How about that?"

"It's perfect," said Clyde and Duke at the
same time.

"Now we have to find decorations for it. Don't
anybody come back until you have something,"
commanded Augie.

Once more, the brothers scattered.

Augie had a habit of sneaking through a
broken floorboard in the bunkhouse, where
he listened to the ranch hands' stories.
He knew that Indian Joe left his string of
coral and turquoise beads on the washstand
while he slept. Augie thought the beads
would be prettier than popcorn strings
hanging on their Christmas cactus.

Quietly, he climbed up on the stand.
Having poor eyesight like all armadillos,
he had to look closely to find the necklace.
Then he poked his nose through the loop and
lifted it off the stand. With it dangling around
his neck, he scooted off.

On his way back to the cactus, he nearly ran into Cook's dinner bell, which had come untied and fallen on the ground. Grabbing the piece of rope in his mouth, Augie dragged it along with him. Cookie would be mad when he tried to call the ranch hands for grub, but Augie planned to return the bell and the necklace as soon as Christmas was over. Those cowpokes didn't need much calling anyway. As soon as they smelled coffee brewing, they came running.

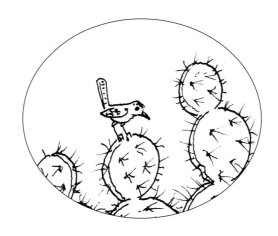

Clyde, nosing around the Jarretts' back porch, spotted little Samantha Jarrett's old sunbonnet in the trash can. He pulled off its yellow ribbon ties and the silk bluebonnets from its crown and then headed back to the cactus.

Clyde had just finished arranging the flowers among the joints of the cactus when he saw Augie coming.

"Look! I found bluebonnets," called Clyde.

"Good job," said Augie. He looked for the best spot to hang the necklace and the dinner bell. Then he let Clyde climb up on his back so he could loop the yellow ribbons over the cactus. Clyde didn't want the ribbons to blow away, so he hooked them on the prickly thorns. "Ouch," he cried, when one of the sharp thorns stuck his front foot.

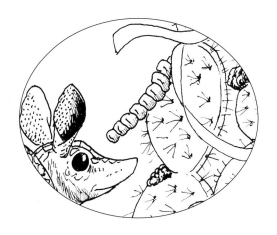

The next one to return was Bud, proudly displaying a large rattle from a rattlesnake.

"Oh, Bud, you're so brave!" said Clyde.

"Well, uh." Bud stumbled over his words and shuffled his feet. "The snake was already dead."

Clyde laughed at his brother.

The rattle made a soft clickety-clack sound when it jiggled in the breeze.

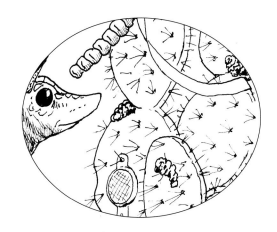

"I have some other stuff," said Bud. He hung a red reflector, which had fallen off the foreman's pick-up truck, better known in these parts as a "Cowboy Cadillac." Next he held up a string of red chile peppers.

"Oh, pretty!" Clyde exclaimed. "Where did you get these?"

"On the old farm road. They must have fallen off somebody's truck on the way to market."

Augie and Clyde helped Bud separate the peppers and hang them on the cactus needles.

When they finished hanging the peppers, they looked around for their youngest brother. Duke still had not returned.

"I hope he's not in trouble," said Augie. "He's always hanging around where it's dangerous."

"Do you think we should try to find him?" asked Bud.

"Let's wait a while longer." Augie tried to be patient with Duke, the mischief maker, but sometimes it wasn't easy.

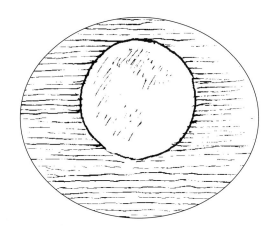

Just as the nighttime breeze began to softly whistle, Duke appeared, dragging Jody Jarrett's saddlebag behind him.

"We were afraid something happened to you," scolded Clyde.

"I went to the stables," Duke panted. "Look what I found."

His brothers took the heavy bag. "How did you carry this by yourself?" Bud asked.

"I'm tough!" Duke lay down to catch his breath while his brothers dumped the bag's contents.

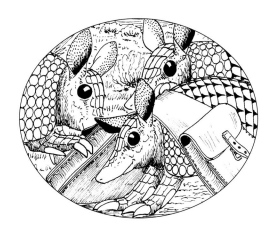

The armadillos were silly with happiness when they saw what was inside. The bag contained a small, wooden longhorn bull Jody's papa had carved, a picture-card of a howling coyote, a horseshoe thrown by Jody's pony, and a belt buckle made in the shape of the Alamo. Duke's objects got special places on the Christmas cactus.

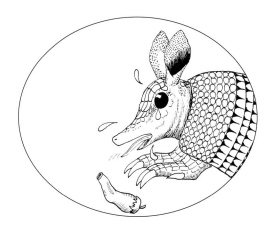

"You have to return these things when we're done with them," said Augie.

Duke curled his upper lip and stared at his brother. "I know that. I'm no dummy."

Standing on his hind legs, Duke plucked one of the red peppers and bit into it. It was hotter than a prairie fire.

Duke ran as fast as he could to the rain barrel at the ranch house and dunked his head.

His brothers laughed as he sprinted away.

"Bet you won't do that again," called Bud.

The armadillos studied their decorated cactus with the bright moon shining on it.

Bud sighed with disappointment. "It doesn't look like the one in the big house."

"Something is missing," added Augie.

Clyde fluffed his yellow ribbons. "Well, I think it's beautiful. A real Texas-style Christmas tree."

The armadillos, tired from their Christmas tree adventure, settled into their burrow and quickly fell asleep.

While they dreamed of Christmas, a cowboy rode by. He was surprised to see the decorated cactus. It reminded him of Christmas trees from his boyhood, and since he had been feeling so lonely, he bunked down beside it.

Just before dawn, the cowboy rose to get back on the trail. But before moving on, he placed something of his own on the armadillos' cactus.

When a ray of light shone on Augie's face, he peeked out of one eye. Then, opening the other, he raised his sleepy head. "Wake up everybody," he shouted.

The armadillos sat up, one by one. They rubbed their eyes and stared in amazement. A gentle sandstorm had come along during the night and left a layer of gleaming white grains covering the cactus and filling its grooves. It stood like a scrumptiously frosted birthday cake.

Most amazing of all was a shiny silver spur on top of the cactus. The rising sun bounced off the spur-star in bright rays.

The armadillo family gathered around the cactus to gaze at the wondrous sight.

"It's the most beautiful Christmas tree in the whole world," gasped Duke.

"That's what was missing," said Bud. "The magical star. Just like the star of the first Christmas."

'Dillo Discoveries

- The armadillo is the state mammal of Texas.

- There are about 20 kinds of armadillos, but the only type found in the United States is the 9-banded armadillo. Despite its name, this type of armadillo can have 7 to 11 bands around its middle.

- When female armadillos reproduce, they always give birth to 4 identical babies of the same sex.

- Armadillos are nocturnal or crepuscular. This means they sleep during the daytime and are active at night or in the twilight hours.

- Armadillos are so sensitive to cold that they may die if a cold spell lasts more than a couple of days.

- Because they have very poor eyesight, armadillos rely on their sense of smell to locate food.

- A cousin to the anteater, the armadillo can eat more than 40,000 ants in one meal.

- An armadillo can hold its breath for as long as six minutes. This comes in especially handy while digging.

- Contrary to popular belief, the 9-banded armadillo cannot roll itself into a ball to protect itself from predators, such as wolves, coyotes, and bobcats. Only the 3-banded armadillo can do this.

- Nine-banded armadillos are the only species of armadillo that can swim. In shallow water, they can even walk or run along the bottom. To cross deeper or broader stretches of water, the 9-banded armadillo will float by inflating its stomach and intestines with air and then will paddle like a dog.

Visit www.ENCHANTEDBOOKS.com for links to fun websites with more armadillo facts.